The Eric Carle Museum of Picture Book Art was built to celebrate
the art that we are first exposed to as children. Located in Amherst,
Massachusetts, the 40,000-square-foot museum is the first in this
country devoted to national and international picture book art.

Visit www.carlemuseum.org

Henry Holt and Company, LLC
Publishers since 1866
175 Fifth Avenue
New York, New York 10010
mackids.com

Library of Congress Cataloging-in-Publication Data
Martin, Bill, 1916–2004.
Brown bear, brown bear, what do you see? / by Bill Martin Jr;
pictures by Eric Carle
Summary: Children see a variety of animals, each one a different color,
and a teacher looking at them.
[1. Color—Fiction. 2. Animals—Fiction. 3. Stories in rhyme.]
I. Carle, Eric, ill. II. Title
PZ8.3.M4189BR   1992   [E]—dc20   91-29115

ISBN 978-0-8050-9536-4
First published in 1967 in a slightly different form by the School Division,
Holt, Rhinehart and Winston
First general book edition—1983
Newly illustrated edition published in 1992 by Henry Holt and Company
Printed in October 2011 in China by South China Printing Co. Ltd.,
Dongguan City, Guangdong Province
10 9 8 7 6 5 4 3 2 1

This special edition was printed for Kohl's Department Stores, Inc.
(for distribution on behalf of Kohl's Cares, LLC, its wholly owned subsidiary)
by Henry Holt Books for Young Readers.
978-0-8050-9536-4 · Kohl's · 0-8050-9536-5 · 123386 · 11/11–3/12

Brown Bear, Brown Bear, What Do You See?

By Bill Martin Jr

Pictures by Eric Carle

Henry Holt and Company · New York

Brown Bear,
Brown Bear,
What do you see?

I see a red bird
looking at me.

Red Bird,
Red Bird,
What do you see?

I see a yellow duck
looking at me.

Yellow Duck,
Yellow Duck,
What do you see?

I see a blue horse
looking at me.

Blue Horse,
Blue Horse,
What do you see?

I see a green frog
looking at me.

Green Frog,
Green Frog,
What do you see?

I see a purple cat
looking at me.

Purple Cat,
Purple Cat,
What do you see?

I see a white dog
looking at me.

White Dog,
White Dog,
What do you see?

I see a black sheep
looking at me.

Black Sheep,
Black Sheep,
What do you see?

I see a goldfish
looking at me.

Goldfish,
Goldfish,
What do you see?

I see a teacher
looking at me.

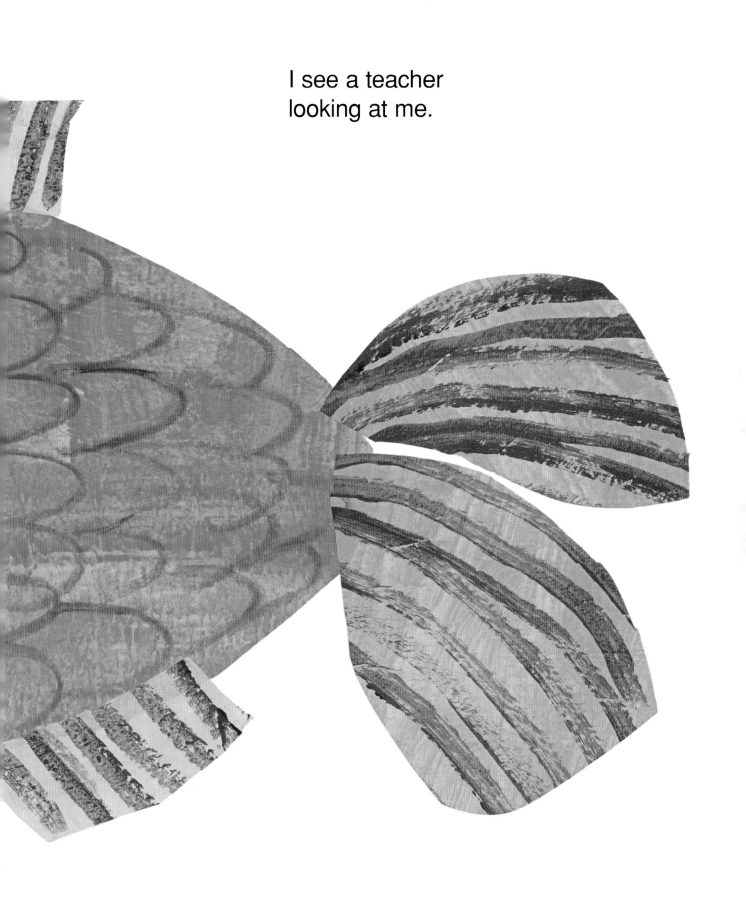

Teacher,
Teacher,
What do you see?

I see children
looking at me.

Children,
Children,
What do you see?

We see a brown bear,

a red bird,

a green frog,

a black sheep,

a goldfish,

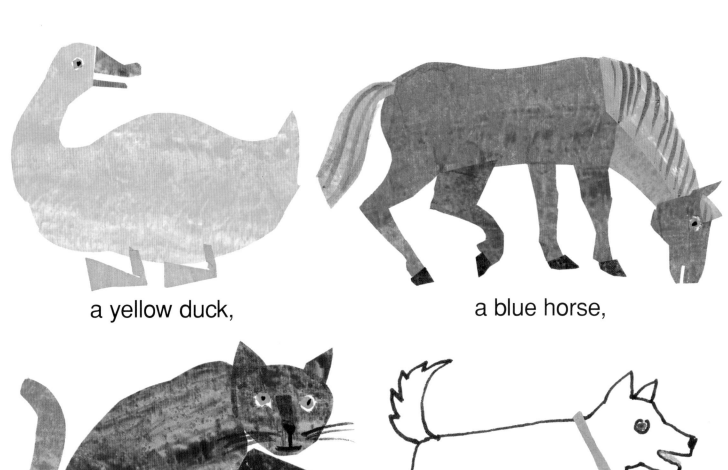

a yellow duck,

a blue horse,

a purple cat,

a white dog,

and a teacher
looking at us.
That's what we see.